MW01228861

1

STAGES:

David's Dance

Written by A. Sebastian McNeil

Copyright

Stages: David's Dance

Copyright© 2023 By A. Sebastian McNeil

Published By
Wonderful Wellness Xperience, L.L.C.
Wonderfulwellnessxperience@gmail.com

Book cover by: A. Sebastian McNeil

Printed in the United States of America
ISBN:9798386235819

Table of Contents

Table of Contents (cont.)

Prologue

The cop was running my ID when two masked men smashed the windows to the passenger-side door.

Glass exploded, and I instinctively covered my face.

Here's what they don't tell you in movies: glass shattering is loud. In movies or TV shows, glass breaks with all the resistance of sugar crystal, which is basically what the fake glass is made out of. It has all the resistance of snapping a toothpick.

But real glass? Shattering right by my ear? It was a louder than a firework. It was like being knocked upside the head. My heart jumped to my throat, and I yelped.

The salty, humid Miami air hit me, and heat rushed into the truck. Cars and trucks passing on the highway zoomed past, making the truck sway with the force of their speed.

A gloved hand reached through the now-broken window and grabbed the bag that had been riding shotgun. I knew it had been stupid to put the bag right in the front seat with me, but I had been in a rush. Whipping the shoulder strap over his head, he revved the engine to the sleek Ducati he was riding and sped off.

The other guy, wearing a mask, rushed around to the driver's side and yanked the door open. He grabbed my arm and hauled me out.

"Move it!"

The cop glanced up from his patrol unit at the noise.

We jumped on the back of the second Ducati, a twin to the first. The guy no more than twisted his wrist to change gears and we were off. I didn't even have time to glance behind me to know that the cop's tires had been slashed.

As I settled onto the leather seat of the bike, for a split second I had a moment of doubt about this whole operation. I wondered whether I was in over my head, whether I should have ever accepted the job from Diamond, or even set foot in that damn club in the first place.

But the moment passed as soon as the driver lifted his foot from the road, and we were flying. Warm, moist air blew hard against my face, mixed with the smell of diesel, greasy fast food, and the coconut trees of Miami Harbor. The high-pitched whine of the engine grew more frantic as the driver changed gears, blasting through the speed limit like every other driver on the I-95.

Zigzagging through the traffic, horns honked and middle fingers extended as we blazed past. Instinctively, I gripped the driver harder; I ain't a bitch, but I wasn't about to become a smear on the pavement, either. Going that fast, the wind seemed like it was trying to rip me off the bike. I squinted to keep bits of debris out of my eyes, and tears stung. The world became a watery blur.

Suddenly, I heard the blare of a siren.

"Step on it!" I yelled over the thunderous wind and noise of the engine.

The vibrations of the bike traveled up my spine and into my skull as the speedometer crept past 100. The siren grew louder. We were going so fast that I didn't want to look behind me. All I could do was focus on the black river of asphalt stretching out before me.

So. I bet you're wondering how the fuck I came to be here, right?

Chapter 1 - Fresh Out

All I wanted was to be a football star.

As I sat in the coach's office, looking around at the maroon and black of the team's uniforms, I could picture exactly how I would look in my uniform, how the stadium lights would reflect off my polished helmet, and how my tight pants would make all the ladies scream. Cause I had a great ass. (*Just being real.*)

"You keep your grades up, and you'll go places, kid," said the burly, pot-bellied coach in front of me. His face was nearly as red as his carrot-top head. I slightly resented being called kid, as I was twenty-three, unlike most of the other fresh-faced eighteen-year-olds running around, but it was better than being called son.

He reached over and shook my hand, then we both stood up. I couldn't help the wide grin that spread across my face. My future was set. I had just gotten out of the military, I had managed to attract the attention of a couple of football scouts, and I had my pick of colleges to go to. With my quick feet, I was a shoe-in for quarterback; coupled with my military background, they were practically begging me to join their teams. I went where I was offered a full ride.

"Yes, sir," I responded automatically. After four years of drills, getting screamed at constantly, and waking up at the crack of dawn, self-discipline was a rock that I fell back on. Even though I didn't have to anymore, I still woke up at four o'clock just to get my morning workout in. Truth was, I needed the routine; my entire life had been routine until a few weeks ago. When I was lying on my cot in the barracks, cursing the itchy, thin blanket for the hundredth time, I thought I wouldn't miss it, would be damn near overjoyed to finally be free of such a strict schedule. But after I left, I realized I needed something to keep me grounded.

"All right now, you go on up to the registrar's office and get your schedule settled," drawled Coach. "Practice'll begin when the semester does."

After I had gotten my schedule, and plenty of things with the university logo splattered across them—t-shirt, plastic water bottle, even a beer coozie, I walked back across campus to my car, breathing in the fresh morning air, feeling like I was on top of the world. I had put in my time and my dues in the military, and now it was time to hustle. I knew what I wanted to study: business, with a minor in communications. I wanted to go places, and I knew that I couldn't fool around and waste this opportunity.

As I strolled across the rolling green lawn under the maples and oaks of the campus, checking out the fine architecture and even finer females, I stopped short at my car. Disappointment broke through my excitement as I looked at the crappy, beat-up Pontiac. The fender was hanging on for its life, the seat cushion was ripped in the back, and the window crank on the passenger's side was busted.

I swallowed the guilt pushing up in my throat. I should have been grateful for the hunk of junk, as my granny had given it to me as a present for surviving the military. I should have been thanking the good Lord for such a sacrifice on the part of my dear granny.

But goddamn.

I plopped into the driver's seat, the heat from the summer engulfing me, and twisted the key in the ignition. After a few seconds of flirting with straight-up dying, the engine sputtered to life. I pulled out of the parking lot and drove home.

Gotta fix that, I thought. *Just gotta find some extra cash.*

The military had given me a nice chunk when I left, but I had spent a fair amount on the flight home, putting a deposit down on an apartment, and other expenses. Plus, when I came back my parents needed to fix their roof when a tree branch put a hole the size of a small elephant into it during a storm.

As I pulled up into the driveway, my good buddy from high school, Luke, was leaning against the side of his car, smoking a cigarette. When he saw me pull up, he flicked away the end.

"See they finally let your sorry ass out," said Luke as I got out of the car. "Look at you: already decked out in the colors. Do you bleed maroon yet?"

"What're you doing here?" I asked, as we clasped

hands. "Don't tell me you've been waiting long."

Luke shrugged; he was pretty easy-going. "Nah. Just wanted to see if you would be my wingman at this party tonight."

It only took me a half second to say no.

"Sorry, man, but I don't have anything to wear. All my clothes are raggedy as shit."

Another thing I have to deal with, I thought. *Need to get some new threads.*

Luke sniffed. "I got something you can wear. C'mon, all the babes from that sorority'll be there tonight. And you know they'll put out, once they see your moooves." Luke gyrated his hips like a fool, and I punched him on the shoulder.

"Nah, man, I'm not about to drive up in this piece of shit." I kicked the car tire, then swore as I busted my toe against it.

"Tommy, you gotta come. You need to relax, after

four years of 'Yes, sir,' 'No, sir,' 'Can I lick your ass for you, sir?'"

I laughed. Luke had a point. Most of the officers were cool, but there were a few who could—and sometimes did—make my life hell.

"Just come with me and chill," Luke continued. He slapped me on the chest. "Wear that new football jersey you got, and the ladies will fall into your lap."

Not a bad option, I thought. It was true. There were plenty of times where we could go out when we were off duty, but it was a different story when I had to get up before the sun did.

I would worry about clothes later.

"Sure," I agreed. "Why not?"

I had no idea that agreeing to go to that party would derail everything in my life.

Chapter 2 – Welcome Home

"You gonna be alright to drive?" I asked Luke as we piled back into his car. It was around 2 a.m., and I was about to collapse. The party had been hot, but my granny had twisted my ear before I left and asked if I was going to church on Sunday. I'd probably hate myself come morning, but you never crossed Granny.

"Yeah, yeah," replied Luke. "Just let me finish this smoke."

We were cruising down the road, and Luke had the radio blasting to try to keep himself awake. His eyelids were getting pretty droopy, so I slapped his head.

"Not asleep," he mumbled.

"Your chin's damn near touching your chest," I said. "Pay attention."

I was in no shape to drive. I had knocked back a good amount of liquor from a red plastic cup, and my head spun too much for me to see straight.

Where we were was pretty mountainous, and the road curved with nothing more than a guardrail separating us from a black chasm. The gentle buzzing of the tires on the pavement was making me sleepy, so I closed my eyes for just a second.

It only took a second.

When I opened them, we were headed straight for the guardrail.

"Luke!" I screamed.

Luke snapped awake, but it was too late.

The car smashed into the guardrail, and time slowed down. The impact jarred me so badly that my teeth shook. As we flew over the edge, I couldn't tell who, exactly, it was that was screaming. The seatbelt jerked against my chest and neck, cutting into my skin. The squeal of the tires rang in my ears. Nothing but a wide, gaping eternity opened up under us.

Then, that deep, hellish pit was over us. Some part of my brain registered that the car was flipping. My stomach rolled. I was strapped to a hellish roller coaster, not knowing which way was up or down. Three, four spins, faster and faster. I was too scared to even be sick. I wondered in that moment whether I would die.

But the car slammed into something; something horrible scraped against the metal. We jerked to a stop. I knew I wasn't dead, 'cause everything hurt too much. The world was still spinning, over and over, even though we were motionless.

I tried to take a breath, but my lungs wouldn't expand. I coughed, clutching the awful thing pressing against my neck. My hands shook as they reached around to undo the seatbelt. I looked wildly around. Tree branches were trying to claw their way into the car. Glass lay shattered everywhere. I glanced to the driver's seat.

Empty.

"Luke!" My voice was raw and scraped the back of my throat. "Luke!"

Observe. Orient. Decide. Act. OODA.

All my training from the military ignited.

Observe. I looked around me, trying to remain calm.

By a miracle, the car had landed in a tree.

Orient. I was suspended about twenty feet in the air.

Decide. I needed to get the hell out of the tree, before the car shifted and pulled me toward my early death.

Act. I began to climb out of the car. My mind was racing, but I couldn't make myself move fast. Adrenaline pumped through my body, but getting out was like crawling through mud.

When my feet touched the ground, my legs gave out underneath me.

Find Luke.

I sat up. There was no time for pity or whining or crying. I had to find my friend. My head spun faster than a washing machine, but I made it to my feet. I scanned the embankment, but I didn't see any sign of him. I started walking, back up to the highway. Something in the back of my mind said that something hurt like hell, but everything hurt. I was alive, and that was all that mattered.

"Help!" I screamed to anyone who might be around.

But at 3 a.m., the only reply was the whisper of passing vehicles.

I started running, half-limping, and made it to the nearest gas station. There was a couple pumping gas, and they were eager to help. They called 9-1-1 and handed me the phone.

"Nine-one-one, where is your emergency?"

The voice cut through my mounting panic.

"Off the 85, about a mile before exit 65. We're down the embankment. Hurry!"

I hung up the phone, then raced back to the site of the crash, looking for Luke. Pain was building in my right foot, shooting up my leg, but I didn't register it. My sole focus was on finding Luke.

As I hobbled up, I saw the smashed guardrail, the metal twisted, and bits of car strewn everywhere. Out of the darkness, a spot of bright red was slowly making its way up the embankment.

"Luke!"

I tried to run faster, but my body was quickly giving up on me. I had been running, literally and figuratively, on pure adrenaline.

I rushed to his side. He was pretty torn up. His jacket was ripped, mud covered his face, and his leg looked useless under him. It was probably broken.

He was alive.

"I got an ambulance coming for you," I said. My heart was pounding against my chest. "Your leg's not looking so good."

Luke's face was drained of blood. He gritted his teeth and managed to choke out, "Your foot's not looking too great either."

It was only then that I looked down at my feet. My right shoe, which was normally white, was now dark red. I sat down, fighting the black that hovered around the edges of my eyes. I carefully peeled my shoe away. When I saw what had happened to my foot, I passed out.

Chapter 3 – Bad News

A week later, I was sitting in the doctor's office. Placards

of awards and achievements dotted the walls. I was sitting

in a chair that had a cushy bottom, but the frame was hard

and dug into my back. It was as though even the chair was

trying to bring me comfort, but all the while telling me I

had better not get too comfortable. My foot was currently

in a huge cast, and it still hurt like hell, despite the pain meds they had given me. I wiped my hands on my jeans, trying to calm my mind. The doctor was about to tell me the extent of the damages to my foot and how long it would take me to recover. I hated starting the season off on the wrong foot with Coach, but as long as I got to play some during the season, I would be happy.

The door clicked open, and a tall woman entered. Her gray hair was cinched tightly in a bun at the base of her neck.

"So sorry to keep you waiting," she said, striding over to her desk.

"Not a problem, ma'am," I said, wiping my hands on my jeans for the tenth time. "How long until I can play football?"

She winced and didn't meet my eyes. That was when I began to worry.

Slipping out the x-ray from the large, white folder, she said, "You've sustained some pretty heavy damage to

27

your talocrural joint." She clipped the x-ray up to the screen, where the black-and-white images made no sense to me. All I saw was my foot. "The posterior malleolus, in particular, took the biggest hit. You'll have to have a few months of therapy." She pointed to the area with a laser pointer.

"Months?" That was a blow.

I might not play a single game this year.

"So when can I start playing? This season? Next season?"

The doctor bit her lower lip and cleared her throat. "Well, that's what I'm trying to tell you, Mr. Smalls. The damages are pretty severe." She leaned forward and dropped her voice. "You'll be able to play recreationally, but any chance at professional football is currently off the table."

My eyes zeroed in on the x-ray. All my hopes for college, for playing football, were suddenly sucked away, as quick as a vacuum. And all because of that black-and-white image of bones.

I shook my head. "Ma'am, there's got to be something. I start this semester. I have to play football. I have a scholarship and everything."

The doctor tucked a nonexistent strand of hair behind her head. "I'm sorry. I really am. With proper physical therapy, you'll regain full use of your foot and leg. But professional sports …" She closed her eyes and shook her head.

I suddenly stood up. I had to get away. I grabbed my crutches and hobbled out as fast as I could, hating the very fact that I had to use them in the first place.

Damages are pretty severe …

Any chance … off the table …

If I could have run, I would have. As it was, I had to endure strange looks from other patients as I angrily gimped my way out of the hospital and into the parking lot, where my parents were waiting to pick me up. I couldn't

drive, not with a busted right foot.

When I got into the car, my mom asked if I wanted

to talk about it.

"No."

We were silent the whole ride home.

Chapter 4 – Nice Moves

A few months later, I finally had the damn cast off. I was going to classes, but fighting with the registrar. Since my full ride based on football had gone to shit, they told me that I had to pay up tuition somehow. I had managed to pay just enough with my G.I. Bill but they were starting to hound me for the rest.

I was laying on my bed, deep in my thoughts. I had a mound of homework that I needed to do, but I couldn't summon the energy to even look at it.

The ceiling fan spun above me, clicking. As I

watched it, I hated the fact that I couldn't play football. I hadn't been to a single game that season, even when my friends invited me to go. I just couldn't stand to see someone else playing what should have been my position.

I glanced at my foot. I had learned to appreciate the simple act of walking again, but every time I thought about my future in football spiraling down the drain, my chest tightened.

Get up, soldier. Move your ass.

Still, I didn't move from the bed. I needed to get out. The therapist had told me that it was my last day, and that I could essentially go on about my normal life.

Ha. Normal. Normal is football. Normal is getting a scholarship and going on to be the next superstar entrepreneur.

As I watched the fan circle around and around, my thoughts spun with it, until my brain finally clicked on a thought. I could either lay on the bed all day and feel sorry for myself or I could get my ass up and go to a club. Maybe the music would be loud enough that I wouldn't have to think anymore. I wouldn't have all these damn thoughts crowding my head.

I reached over and picked up the phone. A few missed calls in my face.

Called Luke.

"Goin' out tonight. You in?"

A few hours later, "Summertime" was bumping through the speakers of a club downtown. The smell of stale beer mixed with weed and cigarettes. The drink was cold in my hand, contrasting with how damn hot it was inside. Going to the club had helped; I didn't have to think about football, my foot, tuition, or anything. Nothing but a hot body in front of me and how I might take her home.

I had just taken a break from a dance battle, where the crowd went crazy over my moves. It was a strategy that Luke and I had devised: we pretended to start fighting, then erupt on the dance floor. Whoever won usually then had the best choice of the ladies, who always sidled up to us afterward.

I locked eyes with a beautiful woman who had smooth, mahogany skin and lustrous, voluminous curves. I gave her one of my lady-killer grins, and she winked one of her almond-shaped eyes at me.

Perfect.

I was just about to make my move.

However, before I could take a step, I felt someone clap a hand over my shoulder.

I turned around and saw a man who looked like he was trying to be the next Biggie Smalls. He had a white homburg hat on top of his bald head and was decked head to toe in Versace.

"Slick moves you got there," he said. He had a North Carolina drawl.

"Thanks," I said.

He looked me up and down, and not for the first time I was severely aware of the lack of personal style. I had a couple of nice shirts, but they were new when "Rebel Without a Pause" hit the radio for the first time. Still, I held his gaze.

"I'm the owner here, and I've got a pretty big scene. Been in the music business for ten years now, and things are about to get off the ground."

I'll admit, I was flattered that the club owner himself came over to talk to me. I was curious about what he wanted.

He jerked his head over to a table. "Come sit down with us. Got a proposition for you." He waved a hand laden with rings.

I walked over to his table, where he had an open bottle of Cristal in front of him. A few other dudes sat around, surveying the club, keeping an eye on the general scene.

"What's your name?" he asked.

"Tommy," I shouted over the music.

"Look, I've been watching you all night. I could really use you. I've got a label of my own that I'm trying to promote." He handed me a card. It had a southern rap feel to the style, which was pretty bold. Everyone was divided between East Coast and West Coast; all the while, the southern scene was slowly sneaking into the cracks.

"As such, I have a few artists with a couple of music videos coming up. I usually have a group of back-up dancers, nothing too fancy, yet—" he grinned at me over the cigar in his mouth, "—but some dropped out. Couldn't hang with the routine, know what I'm saying?"

I waited to see where Knockoff Biggie was going with this.

"If you wanna earn a couple of extra bucks, I have a job for you. Nothing permanent, you understand, but if you do well enough, I may have some more work for you."

My ears perked up at the thought of some extra cash. Between my medical bills, tuition, textbooks, and piece of shit car that I still hadn't fixed, I had plenty of reasons to say yes.

"Alright. What's it pay?"

"Hundred and twenty-five for the day. Cash. Just a couple of music videos, but you'd fit perfectly with the group."

Getting paid to hang with recording artists and dance? Where do I sign? I thought.

"Deal."

Chapter 5 – Dance, Dance?

Dancing went better than I thought. I showed up in the morning, spent a few hours learning the routine, and then practiced with a group of pretty chill dudes. Even though the rappers were low-key, with not a lot of spotlight, it was still cool talking to them. I wondered if any of them would make it big, and I would have gotten to know someone before they were famous.

It was also pretty easy to balance the work with classes and homework. They always met on Saturdays, and whenever we had any tour dates I came back before the end of the weekend. Touring with them kept me from thinking about my disappointment about football too much, which I liked. Sometimes, I brought my textbooks with me and did some homework in the down time, which got me a few jabs and a "Square" here and there, but I was focused. I wasn't going to fuck up my education.

After touring on and off for about a year or so, the club owner walked up to me again. This time, he was decked out in a white suit, with a gold chain around his neck.

"You've been doing great. You show up on time, you don't bitch about the pay, and you're a quick learner."

"Thanks. I learned not to complain about stupid shit when I was in the military."

The club owner smirked. "Well, it shows." He paused, and I had a feeling he had more to say.

"I underestimated you at first. You're a better dancer than I thought. Would you be interested in earning more than you have been?"

"Sure. More music videos?"

"Not exactly. See, I got a group of ladies coming to the club for a private show. These are classy ladies, and they are willing to buy out the entire club for the night."

"Private show?"

The club didn't have any shows that I knew about, but then again, the club owner was pretty tight-lipped with his private business. All I knew was his music side.

"Yeah ... you see, it's a group of about twenty ladies, and they've booked a few entertainers. One of them had to drop out for tonight, something about his family." He shrugged.

"Entertainers?" I started to laugh. "You mean, like strippers?"

"Sure. You didn't know females are horn dogs, too? Man, they go crazy when they see our dancers shirtless. Can barely keep their hands off."

Then, I really started to laugh. "You mean you want me to work as a stripper? Do I have to do tricks on a pole?"

The club owner sniffed. "Ain't like that. You just dance, take your shirt off; don't worry about your pants, they'll take care of those." He paused again. "You're in good shape, and you can dance. The ladies will love you. Go absolutely crazy."

I wasn't completely sold. *Me, working as ... a male stripper? If my military buddies ever found out, they'd howl.*

The club owner must have sensed my hesitation, because he added, "It'll pay well. I'll pay you a flat fee of five hundred for dancing, then you can keep whatever tips you make."

Five hundred dollars to start? That caught my attention more than the gold glistening around the club owner's neck.

I could finally get the registrar off my back with

that. They were threatening to yank my credits away if I couldn't pay up by their extended deadline. They had given me a few weeks past the normal deadline because of my injury and medical bills, but they were gunning for their money now.

How hard can it be to dance for some horny women? I thought. Even if it was just about the craziest thing I ever heard of, the money called to me. If anything, it would make a good story to tell Luke.

"Alright," I agreed. "Male stripping it is."

Chapter 6 - Rookie

I couldn't believe I was nervous. I had been through basic training, all sorts of hellish scenarios in the military, and a car wreck, but this still had my pulse ticking upward. What would I do onstage?

I sat in front of the mirror, looking at myself. I had driven by the barber to get a line up for tonight, and it looked pretty good. I was starting to grow out my hair, since I always had to keep it short in the Army.

"You'll need a name," explained the club manager when I showed up a few days later. "Something sexy. Something that will make them want to open up their legs and wallets."

I felt completely turned upside down, even more than the Fresh Prince. How did the ladies choose their stripper names? I couldn't be Candy or Heaven.

Angel?

I thought about what I might say. "My name's Angel, and I'll send you to heaven, baby," I said out loud to myself in the mirror.

No, that still sounded too much like a female name.

Magic Johnson? I winked at myself in the mirror. "I got a johnson that's magic."

Too stupid.

I decided to not overthink it and went with Wet Dream.

As I was settling on a name, another dark-skinned brother walked into the dressing room. He looked a bit like Wesley Snipes, but even better looking. He had a few white hairs, but the dude was absolutely ripped. When he walked in, he locked eyes with me.

"What's up?" He came over and shook my hand, which kind of threw me. The man had a serious air about him; his eyes were focused like laser pointers, and he walked with a determination I hadn't seen in anyone before. I could tell the guy had more on his mind than just dancing. When we shook hands, he said, "Name's Diamond. You must be the replacement guy."

Oh, guess we're sticking with stage names.

"Yeah, um, I'm … Wet Dream." Maybe if I said it enough times, it wouldn't sound so damn silly. "Good to meet you."

Diamond gave me a once over, then motioned with his chin. "You in school?" he asked.

I glanced at my business economics textbook and wondered if he'd call me square, too.

"Yeah, I said. Livingstone. Studying business," I said, a little on the defensive.

But Diamond nodded his head, looking impressed. "Good. That's real good. Got a good head on your shoulders. You ever danced for ladies before?"

I shook my head and spread my hands. "I actually have no idea what to do."

"Just dance like you're about the give them the best sex of their lives," said Diamond. "For one night, you'll be the best boyfriend they never had, the lover they always want. You're dancing to fulfill their fantasies."

I still was at a complete loss for words. This whole thing felt ridiculous.

"This feels like an acting gig more than a dancing one," I said.

Diamond snapped his fingers. "Exactly. This—" he gestured out to the club area, "—it's all a fantasy. It's made up. They're here because they're bored at home or their husbands treat them like shit, or hell, they just want someone to talk to."

That helped me a little, I guess. As the time drew closer to the actual performance, I started to become more nervous.

Then, the club opened up, and the ladies were ushered inside. The DJ started playing music and introducing the dancers as they went onstage. Some only danced for a song or two, and others lasted longer. I peeked my head out of the dressing room. The women were laughing, cheering, and waving money in the air. There was a mix of Black and white women, and some who looked Latina. One of the dancers was all up on one woman, who was red-faced and screaming wildly, stuffing some bills down his pants.

I couldn't believe I was here. How had I gone from being in the military to being a male entertainer? Still, a grin spread across my face. The energy of the whole club was infectious. It wasn't like a regular strip club, with asses and titties hanging out and greasy men pawing at whatever came their way. This seemed … fun. Laid-back. No one was taking any of it seriously. The women were laughing, which helped set my nerves at ease.

"Next up … Wet Dream!"

Chapter 7 – Wet Dream

Now, I had danced in front of other people before, in the clubs and as a backup dancer, but I had never really been in the spotlight. Not on a stage by myself.

Am I gonna be any good at this? I wondered.

As soon as I stepped out, I knew I shouldn't have been so nervous. About ten or fifteen women had already downed a few drinks, and when I came onstage, they started clapping and hollering even though I hadn't even done anything yet. Besides that, the club was a hole in the wall. The floor was concrete, and looked like it hadn't been swept or mopped in a minute. I didn't need to impress anybody here.

Still, I was in my boxer briefs. The band around my waist felt extra tight, the cotton somehow comforting against my skin. As the bass boomed over us, and some crunk song from the dirty South started pumping, I started to lighten up. The main thing I was worried about was what the hell I was supposed to do with my hands. Still, I was there to act sexy, so I pretended that it wasn't really me going out there, but some guy named Wet Dream who knew exactly what to do.

You are a sexy motherfucker, no, the sexiest motherfucker, and you will make these ladies scream.

The beat was infectious, and as soon as it thumped loud enough to rattle our chests, I started grooving.

Shit, this is easy! I had barely just shaken my hips, and the ladies were already hollering.

As soon as I felt their eyes on me, I started soaking up all their energy and threw it right back at them. I pulled out moves I didn't even know I had. Part of me felt silly, but mostly sexy as hell. When I started moving my hips, some lady reached over, and slapped my ass, then stuck a dollar bill in my briefs.

Whoa, these women are crazy!

After that first tip, it was like the floodgates opened. I would dance for a bit, then another woman would make a grab for my junk but stick in a single.

"That's fine, baby, grab what you want, but leave a little something for me," I said with a wink.

I took to that stage like a fish to water. Something in my mind clicked; this was … actually fun!

Grabbing the woman who had tipped me by the hips, I sat her down in the chair. I grinded on her, like I had seen the other guys do.

"That's right, work it!" said the woman, as she slipped more and more money into my waistband. She had the biggest smile spread across her face, and it made me feel good to make a beautiful woman feel good.

"Now, ladies and … more ladies!" shouted the DJ. That was my cue to start making my way off stage. "Reach those sexy hands deep into your pockets, because tonight's main entertainment will reach deep into yours …"

Whoops and screams tore through the air. I couldn't believe fifteen women could make that much noise. I made my way to the dressing room. Sweat clung to my skin, and my throat was ragged with thirst. I went to a small cooler in the corner and chugged an entire bottle of water in ten seconds flat.

"... Cause you know he's as hard as a ... Diamond!"

The first thing I noticed about Diamond when he strutted onstage was what he wasn't wearing. He had on nothing but some cowboy boots, a cowboy hat, and a G-string. But when he started dancing, I knew this dude was on another level. One move flowed into another; he could sway, bump, grind, and thrust like it was nothing. He danced like he was the sexiest motherfucker alive. He had the ladies practically begging for him. And when he turned around? He was wearing something that looked like an elephant trunk. I had never seen anything like it before.

The ladies are on fire for him, I thought. It wasn't just his moves. Diamond oozed sensuality from every pore. It was the kind of raw power that ladies craved. I had a feeling that he would get the same reaction even if he had been doing something as mundane as brushing his teeth.

After Diamond finished his routine, it was time to basically make the rounds among the ladies to suggest private dances. For a moment, I was a fifteen year old who couldn't look a woman in the eye. Somehow, the thought of asking a woman for money made it all the more awkward. But I gave myself a mental shake. Obviously, we were here to make money, and they were here to give it.

I grinned, stepping out into the fray. Might as well make the most of it.

I managed to score a few private dances, but Diamond was right: this whole show was about making the ladies feel good. Some of them only wanted someone to talk to, and I thought that maybe that would make them want more dances. As I was talking to one of the women, I glanced over at Diamond.

The dude was getting paid. He did dance after dance after dance. He had so much money stuffed in his G-string that he had to slip it into his cowboy boots.

After the show, I started counting up all the money. I had managed to make two hundred bucks from table dances and tips, and my eyes were already bugging out. The paper felt cool and silky in my hands as I counted.

Seven hundred dollars from one night. My crappy car could finally be fixed. I could even go out and buy some new clothes. No way this could have been real. I had just got paid to be sexy, dance some, and get my ass slapped by some beautiful women.

Still, as I glanced at the wad of cash in Diamond's hands, I knew that there was more to this game than just shaking my ass. Diamond knew how to hustle, and I wanted to know everything he did.

He must have seen me with my mouth hanging open, because he walked over.

"Hey, Business Economics, you ever wanna take this to the next level, I'll show you the ropes. Here—" he extended his business card toward me. "I think you got real potential to stay in this game. A lot of people drop out, can't handle it. So what do you say?"

I took the firm cardstock. On it, there was only a picture of a diamond and a phone number.

Get paid to dance and party with women? This was exactly what I needed. Not once the entire night had I thought about football, about the military, about anything other than the ladies and the money. I could handle this and school. Now that I wasn't playing football, I had a lot of time on my hands that I was only too eager to fill.

"Absolutely."

That night, I headed out with a woman I had met at the club for a late-night meal and then back to her house.

She was beautiful, built like that old song "Brick House," and she kept my attention all night with her coy smile.

I felt confident from the club and brought that confidence with me into her bed. And this woman, she made me feel like I was the man.

"Wonderful, wonderful, wonderful," she called out in the middle of our romp in the sheets.

Hearing that word from her dusky voice was ecstasy, and I knew I wanted to hear it over and over. I wanted to hear women calling out wonderful to me.

As we lay in the bed, spent, I asked her why she said wonderful.

"That's what it was," she purred. "And I didn't want to holler Jesus!"

The next day, I became Wonderful.

Chapter 8 – Mr Wonderful

I ended up calling Diamond the very next day. He picked up on the first ring.

"Diamond."

"Diamond, it's Wonderful. I mean, I was Wet Dream, but now it's Wonderful."

"All right, all right, I dig the change. So, you ready to step it up a notch?"

I told him yes, and Diamond said to meet him at the same hole-in-the-wall club where I had first performed the following week. As I drove up in my car, which no longer was wheezing and coughing like it was about to give out, the club seemed almost surreal. It had only been a week, but it felt like a lifetime. As I switched off the ignition, it was a huge relief to know that it would start again. Almost as soon as I had the money from the club, I had fixed my car. I wasn't about to break down on the 85.

Diamond was waiting. "You're late," he said. He glanced at his watch. "I said to meet me here at 1 o'clock."

"It's 1:05."

"So you're five minutes late. You can get money from time, but not the other way around." He motioned his head to his car. A Mercedes C-class with eighteen-inch rims purred in the parking lot. "Hop in. If you're in this for real, you're gonna have to do better than boxer briefs."

Diamond handed me $1,000 and said, "This is a loan." In his old-school-pimp voice, he said, "I want my money, motherfucker." He added, "I'll get my money back from the next two parties."

We drove off. Diamond took me shopping and bought me five different outfits to get me started: a firefighter, a cowboy, a sailor, a tuxedo, and one that didn't look like much of anything, just a G-string with an elephant trunk for my junk.

"What's the pump for?" I asked as Diamond put it in the shopping bag.

He stared at me. Then it hit me.

"You mean—"

"It'll help get you more tips."

After that, he drove us back to the club where he showed me some of the tricks that he had picked up and gave me plenty of advice.

"With the ladies, it's all about that emotional connection. Women are the emotional building blocks of society. But they're tough as shit, so you have to break down that wall. So, when you're giving them a striptease, slow down. Even if you think you're going slow, slow it down even more."

We spent the entire afternoon going over moves and

advice. After that, I knew I had a better chance of picking up women for dances.

At the end of it all, Diamond said, "There's a club in Greensboro we dance at every Sunday. They hire out about fifteen dancers from up and down the East Coast. Now this is a classy place, so you're going to have to practice if you want to earn some real money."

"We?"

"Yes, me and a couple of other guys. I'll introduce you later. You in?"

"Of course."

How could I say no? In some ways, I wanted to be Diamond. He had this … this energy around him. He spent money like it wasn't shit, but from the way he talked, I knew that whatever he spent was an investment. I couldn't say how, but I knew there was something lurking beneath the surface. Diamond was not the type of man to be satisfied dancing at strip clubs all his life. He had an edge to him that told me he had some serious shit going on in the background. And I wanted to be that guy, someone who always had his eye on better things.

I was in love with the whole gig already, even down to the goofy costumes. Little did I know, my career as an exotic dancer would only become wilder.

Chapter 9 – Built For This

Diamond was not joking about the club. It was huge, sparkling, with actual stages, lights, poles, and cushioned seats for the ladies. It was ritzy, glamorous, and a little bit bougie, but I felt like I was about to perform in my first real club. When we pulled up, the scene was already hopping.

I put on my first costume for the night: a cowboy outfit, complete with boots and even a length of rope. I felt the smooth leather of the hat slide down my forehead. Some of this stripping stuff was just plain corny, but I felt like an actor with costumes when I got dressed. Diamond told me that costume changes were necessary, which is why he had helped me out and bought several.

"Spice it up," he said. "Some women prefer one

thing, others another. You have to learn to cater to each of them, but don't get wrapped up in trying to please all of them."

As I was getting ready in the dressing room, Diamond walked up in a cloud of amber musk. I made a mental note to buy some good cologne. Diamond began pointing out all the other dancers.

"We have a small company, if you want to call it that," he explained. "Sometimes we dance with other guys, but these other three are our main go-tos."

He pointed to a brother who was so tall that he seemed like he was about to scrape his head against the ceiling. He was crazy-ripped, built like a linebacker.

"That's Dark," Diamond said.

"I can see why," I replied. The guy was pretty dark-skinned, like sleek ebony.

"Now Dark is cool; he can go a little crazy, but in a good way," said Diamond. "Sometimes he lets the party scene run away with him and he gets caught up."

I nodded as Diamond pointed to another brother.

"That's Entice," he said, as a smaller dude, but no less ripped, stood up and started talking to Dark. "He's ... well, watch your back with him. He's loyal, but only to those he really knows." A frown crossed Diamond's face. "He uses. I keep telling him to lay off that shit, but he's been different ever since he got out of prison."

I glanced at Diamond. "Why'd he go to prison?"

But Diamond didn't reply. He only pointed to someone who had cinnamon skin with jet black, wavy hair and said, "That's Jazz. Jazz is neutral in almost every way. He's like Switzerland. He never bothers nobody; he comes in, makes his money, and bounces."

I stood up; it would take a bit to keep all the names straight in my head, but then again, in the military, we never called anyone by their first names, either. Just their last. Guess learning male stripper names wasn't that much different.

Diamond called everyone over to go over the set. He introduced me to everyone. I bumped fists with Jazz and Dark, but Entice only stared at me.

"All right, here's what we'll do. Entice will go first. Then Wonderful, Jazz, and Dark. I'll finish these ladies off nice."

"Why am I going first?" said Entice.

"Cause you're good to get the ladies riled. Wonderful would be a good transition to Jazz, who'll give them that sensual, Latin love."

Jazz worked out a few steps of samba and laughed.

"We've always gone based on seniority," Entice continued to protest. He threw me a look. "The rookie should go first."

A small, tense silence followed. I didn't need any problems from anyone. I knew plenty about pecking order; the military had hammered in my mind that everyone had to pay their dues. I had been a grunt once, and I didn't mind doing it again.

"Hey, no worries, I'll go first," I said. I looked at Entice and tried to give him a disarming look. "I'll get these ladies so wet, that your job won't be nothing." I nudged Dark, then said, "Plus, I don't need to embarrass myself after all y'all dance."

Dark let out a laugh from his belly. "New guy's got some game!"

"Thanks, Wonderful," said Diamond, but he was looking at Entice. "All right, get out there!"

"What, you mean now?"

"Yes, go!"

"Give me ten minutes."

I grabbed the suitcase I brought and looked through the outfits I'd bought a couple days before. I settled on a black cowboy hat and a skimpy cowboy suit because I was already hot and hadn't even gotten out on the stage with the hot lights and hot women yet.

As Diamond suggested, I had downloaded a few porn on my phone to help improve my situation. I stripped down to nothing but the cowboy hat and went to work with the baby oil to try and elevate the mood.

Damn. I wanted to tell the guys to shut up because I couldn't concentrate, but I knew I would never hear the end of that. So I thought about the girl from last week. She had the richest honey-colored skin and she giggled and tossed her hair, causing her breasts to jiggle every time I touched her side.

That worked like a charm. I threw on the skimpy cowboy suit and headed toward the stage.

As I stepped onto the stage, I felt the shot of adrenaline hit my blood. Two hundred women were crowded around the stage, all hollering, some waving singles; others were taking shots near the bar.

Three poles gleamed when the stage lights swept

over the stage. I climbed the first pole and swung around. I felt right at home. This could have been no more than a playground. I climbed to the top of the sixteen-foot pole until I could touch the ceiling then slid down, grinding at the same time. I hadn't seen any guys do this prior to me, but I'm sure they will after they hear this reaction. As I came down the pole, when I landed, I felt like Superman landing in Metropolis.

But underneath the lights, having literally hundreds of ladies scream for me, I felt like the shit. I was Prince, making the ladies cream. I was Michael Jackson, giving them that thriller. My only thought was how to make these ladies slip a single, or even better, a five or ten, in my waistband. I had my pick of hundreds of women to pull up onstage and grind all over them. I never, in all my life, had expected that I would do anything like this, but here I was, and I loved it.

After my set was done, I went into the dressing

room to towel the sweat off before it stuck. I swiped on more deodorant and asked to borrow some of Jazz's cologne.

"Sure, man," he said, handing it over.

"Thanks. I got a lot to learn about this gig." I slapped some on … but not too much. No one appreciated a walking cloud of overpowering smell.

Dark and Jazz were still performing. Diamond had told me to watch and learn, so I took all the mental notes that I could. I soon realized that my joke about not wanting to be embarrassed turned out to be true.

If I thought Diamond was on another level, the other guys showed me that I had been launched into another league. Every single one of those dudes were turning all sorts of crazy, athletic tricks on the poles, and the ladies were lapping it up. I felt like a total beginner compared to these guys.

They had props and gimmicks that they busted out;

I thought some of them were corny, but they worked. I kicked myself for not using my rope. Some women loved that kinky shit. Still, I watched and analyzed their moves as much as I could. If I didn't want to feel like a rookie anymore, then I had to know how to dance like a male entertainer. I already knew how to dance, but there was an extra element to what these ladies wanted.

After that show, Diamond wanted me to do another party in Virginia with Dark.

I got off the stage around 9 p.m., cleaned up, and packed. Dark finished around 9:30.

Dark said, "Time to hit the road. We got a two-hour hump up this road. Gotta be there before midnight."

"We gotta drive two hours to Virginia for real?"

Dark punched me on the shoulder. "You wanna be a hustler, you gotta hustle."

By the time we had finished, around 1:30 a.m., I was about to collapse. At the second party, I made around

$300 upfront, plus tips, and all the private dances. I was starting to see how stripping wasn't just about dancing. It was catering to the ladies, knowing how to approach them, how to talk with them; what worked for one didn't work for another. Sometimes some of the white women had something ignorant to say, but I was more than happy to take their money. It was customer service, with the military discipline of showing up on time, plus athleticism. I had basically danced for four hours in total that day, more work than I would have done if I had played football.

So when the party was over, I asked Dark, "So are we staying in a motel or something?"

"Nah, we're heading back."

My eyes nearly bugged out of my skull.

"What?"

But Dark just threw me a look and said, "Hop in. I'll drive."

It seemed strange to me, but I was too tired to

argue. I had my hands on nearly nine hundred dollars, the fattest wad of cash that I had ever made in a single day. The night smelled like money and sex, and I had never felt more exhilarated. In two hours, I'm sleeping the day away.

Chapter 10 – Something New

If I had thought ever stripping was easy, the months that followed proved how wrong I was. It wasn't all just dancing and sticking my waistband out for a dollar. Diamond was right. I had to be an actor, a therapist, an athlete, a customer-service expert, and a sex god, all rolled into one.

Meanwhile, I was keeping up with college. The military had prepared me for long nights and early mornings, and I could leave a party at midnight or 2 a.m. on Sunday and be in class at 8 a.m. Monday. I finally paid off the Registrar, in cash. As I counted out each twenty, I couldn't help but smile, knowing that my college education was being paid for by a bunch of horny women. As the money flowed in, it started flowing out: I bought some new clothes, both for myself and outfits for the clubs. When I went to the mall and saw something I liked, I bought it then and there: watches, shoes, CDs, a new stereo. I was smooth and loving it. I knew that, eventually, I would want to save some of it, but for now, I was damn happy just flinging my money around, not caring about price tags.

Still, I wanted to be on the next level. I didn't just want to fix my car; I wanted a new one. I didn't just want to buy a new watch; I wanted a Rolex.

I even told Luke about the whole thing and he started laughing, until he saw my money.

"God damn!" he said. "You make all that by stripping?"

Every show with Diamond was a crash course in the art of male stripping. He was a tough teacher: stern, no-nonsense, and I still couldn't shake the feeling that there was more to this dude than dancing.

For one, he was serious about calling our little group a company. We might do three shows per night, all in different venues in different cities, but that was rare. Still, even if we had only two parties, we had to show up on time, then book it to the next show. However, by the very nature of the gig we might leave the party late; more often than not, the women wanted encore performances, or they wanted just one more dance, or we had to guide their drunk asses to the ATM to pay us. That would make us late to the second party, which would impact the third.

Once, I was riding with him in the Benz, and he practically threw the cell phone at me.

"Call this number," he said, opening the glove compartment and giving me a contact book. He was weaving in and out of traffic like a maniac. "Do not say we're gonna be late."

I dialed the number and a woman's voice picked up. "Where are you?" she screeched. "The women are getting antsy, and there's only so much alcohol they'll drink!"

"Ma'am, we're in town, heading your way," I said in my smoothest voice. I glanced out the window; we were still half an hour away in heavy traffic. "We're just picking something up to make the night a little extra special."

"Get here now!"

I continued to reassure the frantic club owner.

It was at one of these marathon nights that the simmering tension with Entice heated up a little. I had made friends with Dark and Jazz easy enough, but Diamond was right about Entice. He was hard, quick to get jealous, and easily ticked off; I didn't talk to him much and he didn't talk to me either, so we remained in a state of neutrality.

Until South Carolina.

It was going to be a three-party night, and already I was getting my mind, among other things, prepared and ready for all the action. The first party was in Columbia. It

75

was a birthday scene, with about twenty women crammed into a hotel suite. Diamond explained the rotation.

"I'll give you your intro; you dance, then as soon as you finish, you'll do a party with Entice in downtown Charlotte. 10:00 p.m. You two can work out who goes first. Then, it's on to party number three in Statesville at midnight."

As Diamond and I walked up to the hotel room, music poured through the cracks in the door. We were wearing matching police uniforms. Diamond pounded on the door.

"Police! Open up!"

The music cut off immediately.

A striking brunette with honey-colored skin opened the door. Diamond and I pushed our way in, looking serious.

"Now, there have been some complaints," said Diamond. "About some very ... bad ... ladies!" Then, he ripped his shirt off.

The ladies cheered and the music cut on again.

"Are you ready to holler for the dollar?"

Apparently, they were.

Diamond danced the intro, then I came on with my main sequence. I had my trick with a watermelon that the ladies went absolutely hysterical over. I was pretty damn proud of that trick, because I had thought of it myself, but I was saving it for the second party. Then, as soon as I finished, Diamond took the floor again, and I left.

The twenty women blocking the door did not make it easy.

"Stay just a little longer," one of the women said. She wore a slinky, bright red dress, and she was swaying slightly on her feet.

I had to admit, having beautiful women throw themselves at me was like something out of a *Penthouse* fantasy.

"Sorry, baby, next time," I said, gently lifting her hands off me.

She pouted, but one of her friends grabbed her and threw her back into the scene.

It was my turn to drive like a crazy person; as much money as I made doing parties downtown, they grated on me, because I could never find parking at 10 p.m. on a weekend night. After circling the block for about fifteen minutes, I saw a car backing out, and I immediately threw on my signal. I whipped in; I only had five minutes to book it across the road and to the bachelorette party with Entice.

Popping open the trunk, I grabbed the watermelon, but I was in such a rush, I almost dropped it. My heart almost jumped out of my chest thinking about the amount of money I almost dropped on the ground. I almost shit myself imagining losing a $1,000 watermelon.

So there I was, rushing into the hotel with all my props, trying to get myself situated. I ran into the elevator and punched the button five times to make it go faster. In the meantime, I pulled out the pump that Diamond had bought me. I usually waited until I had a bit more privacy, but I was cutting it close to being late. I stuck it down my pants and started pumping away, to get myself ready for the ladies.

When the doors opened, an old, shriveled couple was standing there. As soon as they saw me, the woman yelped.

"Sorry!" I gasped, rushing out of the elevator and down the hall. I checked my watch. Only five minutes late.

Entice opened the door. "About time."

"Sorry," I said. "I'm here."

"Good. You'll go first. Do my intro." He said it as though he were challenging me to disagree.

"That's fine." I was … well … pumped and ready to go. I still didn't mind doing the intros. Some of the dancers could be damn prima donnas, but I liked going first. I loved that my face and body were the very first thing that the ladies saw. I knew that if I got their attention first, then I wouldn't get lost in the crowd, especially if there were ten or fifteen dancers.

I'd already prepped the watermelon ahead of time, so it was ready to go. I'd cut an oval in the watermelon and clean out the insides, one oval on each side. Then, I'd put the pieces back in and wrap the whole watermelon in a towel.

I turned to the ladies.

I pulled out the first piece of watermelon and filled the inside with whipped cream. I also put some whipped cream on the piece I pulled out and started teasing that piece of watermelon with my tongue, then going faster and faster. You could see the women start to squirm in the seats, crossing and uncrossing their legs.

Then, I slid my dick into the hole in the watermelon, started gliding back and forth in the whipped cream. Slower, then faster to the rhythm of the music. The ladies started to actually moan and squeal. As the music built to the climax, I moved faster and faster before finally busting out the other side of the watermelon.

Who knew the secret was a damn watermelon? I thought.

The women pelted me with money from every direction, begging me to take them into a private dance. They were stuffing money into my pockets so fast that I couldn't keep up with it all. I was about to bow out and give Entice the floor, but they kept shouting, "One more! Give us one more!" So I stayed and kept dancing, keeping the party hot.

It wasn't until I glanced at the clock on the wall that I noticed that it was close to 11. I had danced for about forty minutes, and I needed to high-tail it out of there to be on time for the next party.

I introduced Entice to the ladies and made my exit.

"See at the next party," I said to Entice, already throwing my props into my bag.

"Staaaaay," cooed one of the ladies. "Keep dancing." She traced a finger down my bare chest. "I'd like to talk to you after the party."

God damn it, my solider was standing at attention, without the need for the pump, thinking about this beauty in front of me.

As I gave her my apologies, I swore to myself that I would get laid within the next twenty-four hours. But it was on to Statesville for the midnight party. I didn't even have time to count the fat wad of cash that I had made in Charlotte, but it had to be at least a couple of hundred in tips alone.

As I drove along the highway, I fought off the fatigue hovering around the edges of my eyes. I needed to be alert, so I pulled over at a gas station and bought a large cup of coffee and a couple of really pathetic-looking sandwiches. I was so hungry that I practically inhaled them.

When I met Diamond at the next party, he was already dressed and ready to go.

Diamond glanced at his watch. "Excellent," he said. "How did the other parties go?"

I grinned. "Fan-fucking-tastic."

"Good. Keep that energy up. You'll need it."

This party had a different vibe than the others; it was a bachelorette party, and while the ladies were looking for a good time, they weren't necessarily the party animals of the other two groups. The party in Charlotte had been mostly single ladies for a birthday party, but most of these women had boyfriends and just wanted to give their friend a goofy send-off. They weren't looking for anything too raunchy, so I adjusted my dance style and level of handsy-ness to accommodate the mood.

I intro'd Diamond, then after he danced for thirty minutes, he let me have the floor. By the time I had finished dancing, Entice had finished the other party and had made it over to this one, so I introduced him onto the floor.

Around 2 a.m., we finished up the party, and I had the strangest sensation. I wanted to both collapse and felt buzzed. I wasn't sure, but I had a strong feeling that I would walk away from tonight with around a thousand bucks.

As we were all cleaning ourselves up, I said, "Man, tonight was a great night." I stretched my arms overhead and heard my elbows pop.

Entice sniffed. "Yeah, maybe for some of us."

I should have heard the warning in his voice, but I was too hopped up on the energy of the night to care.

"What're talking about? The ladies loved us."

Entice jerked around. "No, the ladies loved you." He stabbed a finger in my direction. "When's Mr. Wonderful coming back? Can we see Wonderful again?"

He made his voice go high-pitched in mocking sarcasm. "You stole the party." He shoved some shorts into his gym bag and zipped it up so hard it was in danger of breaking.

I shrugged. "Come on, man, there's plenty to go around."

Entice barked out a laugh. "Apparently not. I barely got anything from that last party. By the time I danced, they all said they had run out of money!"

Diamond was watching us, following the argument with his eyes, like a tennis match. But he didn't say anything.

A rush of hot glee stole through me. It wasn't my fault if Entice had insisted on me going first.

"Sorry, man, but you wanted to follow seniority."

"Well next time, why don't you save some for the fucking rest of us?"

For a moment, we just stared at each other, feeling the tension between us crackle. I had no way of knowing, but that wouldn't be the last time that Entice and I would

fight. And the next time we did, it would get a lot nastier.

"Enough." Diamond didn't need to yell to command

authority. He turned to me. "Wonderful, know when to stop

dancing and pass the party onto the next person." Then he

turned to Entice. "Entice? Quit being a little bitch."

Entice didn't say anything; he just threw his duffle

bag over his shoulder and stomped out of the room. The

sound of tires squealing out of the parking lot soon

followed.

Diamond let out a huff of air. "Crazy

motherfucker." He seemed to remember that I was in the

room also, because he stretched, popped his neck and said,

"You wanna get something to eat?"

I had burned away the sandwiches and coffee away

a long time ago. The first party seemed like it had happened

last week.

"Fuck yeah, I'm starving."

We pulled over into a twenty-four-hour diner and ordered two giant hamburgers, large shakes, and two baskets of fries. Diamond told the waitress to hold the bacon, since he didn't eat pork. I had never been this hungry, even after football practice.

"You did a good job tonight," Diamond said over the ruins of fries and bits and pieces of burger. He gazed at me intently.

"Thanks," I said, slurping the last of my milkshake.

Diamond leaned over the table. "You know, this was a test for you."

I stopped slurping.

"I wanted to see if you had the endurance for all this. Had the skills. Not everyone does." He leaned back again. "I think you're ready for something new."

Even though it was close to 4 a.m., I had enough neurons firing to have my curiosity piqued.

"You mean like more dancing?"

Diamond wiped his mouth. "Not exactly." He threw down a couple of twenties and stood up. "How about you come with me to Miami next Friday? I'll introduce you to some people."

I had never been to Miami before, but as soon as he said the word, my mind instantly conjured images of sunny beaches, turquoise water, and hot babes.

"Sure."

Maybe I should have asked a few more questions, because what Diamond had in mind was so far beyond dancing that I never saw it coming. But once he told me, I was eager to jump in.

Maybe a bit too eager.

Chapter 11 - Miami

When Diamond drove to up my house on Friday to pick me up, my mouth dropped open. He gripped the wheel of a sleek, black Bentley with the top down. His white cotton shirt was unbuttoned to the second button, and a Cuban hat was perched atop his head.

The motor was humming as I hopped inside. The smooth leather of the seats welcomed me like an old friend. It was cleaner than my pop's Sunday dress shoes.

"Nice ride," I said. I instantly felt like a hotshot, riding in that car. I didn't even have to own it to feel like a boss. For a second, it wasn't jealousy that gripped me but determination. I would do anything to own a car like this in the future.

"Thanks," he said. "It's what I drive when I go to Miami."

Which made me wonder just how many cars Diamond had. We took off down the highway, the breeze tickling the back of my neck. The sun felt great on my face. The sky was the kind of blue you saw in dreams and movies: a perfect, bright day, with clouds scuttling over the sun every once in a while to give us some shade. Diamond cycled through radio stations he knew by heart as he crossed state boundaries. After the parties, it had been a relatively slow week, which was fine with me. We all needed to recover after the three-party endurance run.

We were driving down the 95 when my curiosity couldn't take it anymore.

"So what's this all about?" I asked. "Is this a new gig?"

Diamond didn't say anything for a few moments. Oak trees gradually gave way to palms as we drove farther and farther south. "I'm looking for a new partner," he said. "I think you could be that man."

"For the stripping biz?"

Diamond rubbed his chin, scratching at the beginnings of stubble. "A bit more than that."

I was secretly pleased, but I tried to not let it show too much. "Why me?"

"You're smart," Diamond said instantly. "You're about as green as my weed, but you've got that natural instinct for making money. What you don't already know, you'll learn. You're ambitious. And most importantly—" He deftly changed lanes and eased the pedal toward 90. "I can trust you."

After years of slogging through the military, where I heard men scream how worthless I was, how much of a pussy, how weak, and a screw-up, I almost couldn't believe him. Still, Diamond's words hit something in me, something that I was longing for. In truth, I wanted to be

Diamond so much that I would have signed up for anything that he suggested. It wasn't just the money. He had a focus that I lacked, a determination that was rare. And now, to have him compliment me and practically shower me with praise?

It was just too good.

"Well, what about the other guys? Dark or Jazz?" I swallowed. "Or Entice?"

Diamond sucked in through his teeth. "Jazz doesn't care beyond making his money and screwing. Dark is too much of a party rat. And Entice …"

We passed a sign welcoming us to Miami, and the smell of the sea greeted us as much as the heat did. "I used to trust Entice." The sad thing was that I heard the regret in his voice. "I … I owe Entice. He caught some heat for me. Did a year and a half in a Federal camp. He had every chance to squeal, cut a deal, whatever. But he never did. I trust him as far as not talking, but with money, with my business?" Diamond shook his head.

Something like a warning sounded in my mind. Whatever Diamond had going on, something wasn't legal. I kept silent. The roar of the tires against pavement hummed beneath us.

"Like I said, he changed," Diamond continued. "He was already living hard before I met him. But he doesn't think. He just rushes from one thing to another, always running, never looking back."

As much as I wanted to feel superior to Entice, something about Diamond's words hit something in me. I shifted in my seat and cleared my throat. "So, uh ... why are you looking for a partner now?"

Diamond took a deep breath. "I want out." He was so quiet that I almost didn't hear him over the hum of the wind. "My baby girl's already six. I don't want to miss her life. I want to be there for her and not be a ghost, like my old man was. I've been doing this gig for almost twenty years. It's time." It was the first time I had ever heard anything like … like emotion from Diamond. The man sounded … almost vulnerable.

Twenty years … for the first time, I took a really good look at Diamond. He had the faint edges of lines around his eyes; a stray white hair or two popped up along the edges of his temples. The dude could have easily whupped my ass, but for the first time, I saw a weariness in his body.

"Anyway," he continued. "I've got a lot of things already set up. Stripping is more like a side gig. All I need is someone to take over running it. I'll still keep a cut, but someone needs to coordinate it all. I think that person could be you."

We crossed a huge bridge into the city. The water was so blue that it struck something deep in me. My breath caught in my lungs. The waves were beautiful, with their white peaks cresting, like strings of diamonds against an azure field. The ocean was freedom and expanse. When I looked at it, I had the feeling that I could keep running forever across the surface of the water, and it still wouldn't ever be far enough. It was a haunting, yet exhilarating, feeling.

"So ... you ever gonna tell me what the hell it is that you do, or just pussy-foot around it?"

That earned a chuckle from Diamond. "Just wait."

He leaned over and turned up the radio. "Miami" by Will Smith bumped through the radio, and I felt like it was my personal welcome.

"Did the speakers come with the ride?" I had to yell over the bass. It thumped deep in my chest.

"Nope, got it installed."

God damn, is there anything this dude doesn't own? I leaned the seat back and just enjoyed the sparkling vista of the city.

After taking a scenic drive through Miami, we

pulled up into a section of the city called Boca Raton. As we pulled up to Diamond's apartment complex, something began to nag at me.

No way he pays for this just by stripping, I thought.

The high-rise apartment towered into the sky, along with dozens of others, and hugging along the sidewalk were luxury shops, restaurants, and plenty of ladies in form-fitting dresses. The curved, cultivated drive had a valet, and the building looked so brand-spanking new that each part of it practically gleamed: the sun-bleached stones, the gigantic windows, and even the fountain bubbling out front looked like someone scrubbed them twice a day.

Diamond parked behind a generic-looking box truck, and he let out a distinct huff of annoyance.

"Stay here for a sec," he said and got out.

He walked up to the box truck, and the driver got out. They stood for a few minutes talking, and I wasn't really paying attention to them. Traffic honked as it flowed by, and the cry of seagulls was never very far away. The aroma of pulled pork sandwiches was drifting from a food truck parked nearby, making my mouth water.

But not as much as the lady window shopping. My eyes were fixed on her fat ass and skinny waist, and I was deep into thinking about what I would do with this female when I overheard Diamond say, "I told you not to come here."

There was just enough warning in his voice to break my reverie.

I glanced to the sidewalk where they were standing. Diamond quickly slipped him something, and just like that, the driver hopped in the box truck and drove away.

When Diamond came back, he said, "Last time I ever pay that fool. Can't trust anybody. This is why I need you."

I didn't understand anything that was going on, but I was wise enough to keep my mouth shut. If Diamond said to wait, then I would. I would prove that I could be his man.

He started the engine again and pulled up to the valet, who he greeted by name and slipped a couple of bills.

When we walked into the building, the AC that hit my face was so cold that I immediately got goose bumps, a welcome relief from the heat outside. I tried to not look too corny, but my eyes wanted to bug out of my head. The sheer luxury of the place was getting to me. Glass chandeliers hung from the ceiling, and there was an honest-to-god footman in the elevator. As we rose, the elevator moved so fast that my stomach was left behind, and my ears popped after a few seconds.

"Penthouse, sir," said Elevator Guy.

Diamond tipped him, too. As the doors opened, I was unprepared for what I saw.

Floor-to-ceiling windows looked out over the glistening Miami harbor. The ceiling was so tall that my footsteps echoed when I walked across the floor. The furniture was all white and probably cost more than what I made in an entire year; it contrasted with the black marble floor, shot through with golden seams. Diamond even had classy art decorating his walls, everything from African Madonnas to still-life portraits.

There was already a group of people sitting on the huge couches with half-filled glasses of liquor. We walked up to them. There were about six or seven, a mix of men and women. The ladies had jewelry dripping from their ears, throats, and wrists. They looked like they had just stepped out of *Ebony* magazine.

"What's good?" said one of the men. One of the women wiggled her fingers at me.

"Take a seat. Relax. We got a big show tomorrow." Diamond motioned to the bottles of liquor. "You want Machallan or Hennessey?"

"Uh, Henny."

"My man," said a dark-skinned brother, who gave me a fist bump. He was lounging between two ladies. One had a beautiful Afro with giant hoop earrings, and the other was light-skinned with dyed red hair. Usually I didn't like anything unnatural, but she pulled it off. There were a few other women, all drop-dead gorgeous. "Don't know why you bother with the expensive shit, Diamond."

Diamond poured my glass and handed it to me. "Ain't all of us got juvenile taste, M."

The man called M only shrugged. "Can't tell the difference. Especially with that dank you got. Speaking of which ..." He leaned forward and took another crystal container filled with familiar green buds. When he opened the lid, the gas was so loud that it immediately filled the room. He started rolling one up for all of us.

The lady with the Afro fixed me with a grin. She rubbed the seat beside her. "Come on, baby, don't be shy."

"Oh, I've never been shy." I dropped down on the

cushiest seat my ass ever had the pleasure to sit on. She laid a manicured hand on my shoulder. Her nails felt good against my skin, as they rubbed slowly back and forth. "Tell me about yourself."

The Hennessey bit as I took a swig, and the white tendrils of smoke curled from the joint being passed around.

For the rest of the afternoon, I chatted up the ladies and swapped bullshit with M, Diamond, and the rest of the guys there. I wondered how Diamond had this much money, how I fit into all of this, and why the box truck had been sitting outside. My fight with Entice was miles behind me, and I was luxuriating in the attention of the women, feeling the warmth of the Hennessey as it bloomed in my stomach.

Diamond and the other guys were talking, and I was observing some, but mostly relaxing. If Diamond wanted to bring me into all this, if this was how much he had going on, then I couldn't wait to get into the action. The strict, disciplined part of my mind sounded off a small warning, but I just drowned it with more Henny. As the sun went down and lit up Miami with blazing orange and red, me and the ladies went exploring around Diamond's suite. As it turned out, he had plenty of spare bedrooms, all of them with California king beds. We shut the door, locked it, and did what grown folks do, when grown folks are rolling and high on money and life.

Chapter 12 – Truck Driver

"You want to pay me $2,000 to drive a truck?"

It was Saturday morning, and Diamond had courteously but firmly escorted the ladies out of the room so we could get down to business. I admired the curve of their delicious asses and was sorry to see them go so quickly. My confidence from stripping had translated to the bedroom, and I felt like a rock star giving it to the women.

I dragged myself out of the bed, splashed some water on my face, and plopped down on the couch. The buttery sunlight filled the living room; the drinks and cigarette butts crushed from the night before still littered the table.

Diamond had shown me his lifestyle, and I was soaking up every part of it. If he wanted me to be a chauffeur, then I would drive his royal ass anywhere. Now the question hung in the air.

He didn't say anything, and I had come to expect a lot out of his philosophical pauses. That was when I started to feel that there was something very, very different about this truck.

"The thing is that this particular vehicle will be carrying a package. It'll be your first test. I gotta know that I can trust you with this."

"Yeah, man, I got you. Whatever you need."

Diamond shook his head, as if I still didn't get it. "Look. This ain't dancing. This is some real shit." Then he bored into me with his laser eyes, and suddenly, my grogginess vanished. Everything started clicking into place.

The money. His cars. A sweet apartment in Miami. A truck with a special package.

"I need to know that I can trust you," he repeated.

If Diamond had told me to jump off a bridge at that moment, I probably would have. If he had told me to swallow a bee, I'd have placed honey on my tongue. The more Diamond showed me of his lifestyle, the more I hungered for it. He had everything that I wanted: cars, women, a sweet pad, and money that he could be generous with. But it was more than that; Diamond was offering me a chance to escape the ordinary life I was living. Even if my world had been rocked by stripping, it was still within the confines of normal. Simple. Show up, work, go home. Repeat. I needed something more.

So the warning that I would soon be a mule, transporting drugs, only registered as much as a mosquito bite. It should have been a gunshot.

"You can trust me." I had never been more serious about anything in my life. "What kind of shit is it?"

"Blow."

I nodded my head, as if I did this all the time. "Where does it come from?"

"Best if you don't know too much. I don't even know that much. I don't sell, just provide the infrastructure."

He leaned forward. "The rules are simple. Drive carefully and all the way until you get to the city. No stops. Not one mile over the speed limit." He tapped the table for emphasis. "Always use your blinker. Don't run red lights. Don't even run yellow."

My heart was pounding. It wasn't fear so much as excitement. Somewhere my rationality told me I should be sweating over something so illegal. If I were caught, I wouldn't be any better than Entice. My life would be ruined.

And yet …

Diamond handed me a stack of hundreds. "This is for the first run."

My fist curled around the money. "What happens if I get pulled over?"

Diamond flashed his eyes at me. "You don't get pulled over."

"Come on, man, you know driving while Black is a crime."

Diamond's mouth quirked. "We have a contingency plan. You'll get a fake license, but all the insurance is up-to-date. In the event that an officer pulls you over, be cool. Polite. Give him whatever he wants. Two of the guys will always be following you on motorcycles. If things get serious, you'll give a signal out the window. They'll come, slash his tires, then come around and do a smash-and-grab. Hop on the bikes. While the cops are chasing their tails, you'll be long gone."

I took a deep breath but leaned back against the couch. As long as there was a backup plan. "Nothing to it, then."

Diamond smiled. "You do this, prove yourself, then things could work out very well for both of us." He glanced at his watch. "Let's get to the club. The others are probably already there."

My life was now a roller coaster, with ever-growing hills. And something that would throw me into a loop was right around the corner.

Chapter 13 – 1ˢᵗ Run

The club in Miami made all of the other clubs look like

truck stops. It was enormous and classy with curving lines,

waitresses in skimpy, sparkling white dresses, and velvet

couches. The lighting was professional, and there were

about fifteen small stages dotted all around the space. The

interior decorating was lavish, done in dark purples and

blacks. Bottles of expensive liquor and champagne lined

the back walls; a cigar room stood proudly in the corner,

and complete bottle service came ready for any customer

with a black credit card. All of the waitresses looked like

they were models, and they probably were. Everyone in Miami was hustling, trying to make it big. A line stretched for blocks, filled with more women who were dying to get it.

I was just about to order something for all of us, when Diamond said, "No drinking. Tonight is strictly business. We'll head back to North Carolina tonight, and you'll be driving the truck."

"All right," I said, eyeing the women in the club. They looked like they came from all over the world, every color of the human rainbow. There were women with honey-colored skin and full eyelashes who looked Latina, tiny Asian women, women with straight blonde hair and blue eyes, ebony-skinned women who looked more Indian than anything else, and everything in between.

"I'm serious, Wonderful. Keep focused tonight."

We changed and hit the floor.

It was more like a huge party than anything else.

The DJ was hot and knew his stuff; the waitresses were professional and quick; and the women came wild and ready. They were constantly ordering bottles of champagne as they celebrated birthdays, bachelorette parties, newly divorced parties, or just partying for the hell of it.

Besides our normal group, there were about twenty other dancers spread out in the club. We took turns on the small stages, and for the rest of the time we hustled. With about five hundred women in the club, there was a lot of money moving around. These ladies were ready to spend. Instead of the typical dollar or two, I had ladies stuff five-, ten-, even twenty-dollar bills in my waistband just as onstage tips. Jazz and I would often hook up with a table and spend two or three songs with a party group giving all of the ladies dances, then moving on when they wanted a break.

I was on rotation on a stage when I saw the most beautiful woman I ever had in my life. In a sea of gorgeous women, she stood out. She looked like she came from the islands or something, with that exotic glow about her. I couldn't take my eyes off her. She was dancing with a group of friends, and when she glanced up at me, we held each other's gaze for a full five seconds.

As soon as I was done with my set, I started working my way toward her. If I didn't at least say hello, I would have been a fool.

Chapter 14 – New Lead

For the next eight months to a year, things were going smooth and life was awesome. Living in Miami, Lynette kept coming to shows when she could but it didn't matter. We spent weekends together whenever we could and sometimes never made it out of bed.

We continued to do shows and made the Miami run a couple of times a month. I was floating easy with Lynette, cash, and smooth runs. The crew had everything down and knew exactly what to do. We would always leave right after the club closed. I drove the truck, Diamond had the lead, and the guys on motorcycles rode in back. We had almost no problems at all.

The one problem we did have was Entice. I knew Diamond didn't trust him anymore, and Tice knew it too. He wasn't getting the same attention from Diamond anymore, and he expressed his displeasure through his attitude. He missed shows or was late. He acted unprofessionally. He grated on everyone's nerves, but he was always right on time for runs. Our patience was wearing thin and we talked about possibly cutting him out. We still needed him though, so we didn't.

At the club one night, Diamond said he wanted to hold a crew meeting after hours since we didn't have a run after. We gathered at Diamond's house and were chillin' in his living room. He brought out a couple bottles of liquor and some glasses and offered everyone a drink.

"I really appreciate all of the hard work you guys have put in for the past few months. We have a really good thing going here, and I don't want that to end," Diamond said. "With that said, it's time for me to take a step back, switch directions, put my focus on my family."

No one said a word, but the fellas all looked at each other and shifted around a bit in their seats. I'm sure everyone was thinking exactly the same thing I was: so what happens now? Entice sat up a little straighter in his chair, probably thinking that since he was Diamond's right-hand man for so long, he would be the new Boss.

"We gonna keep doing runs? Miami?" Entice asked.

"Everything will continue just the way it has been," Diamond said. "Same routine, same club, different lead."

It looked like Entice was starting to say something, but Diamond cut him off before he got a word out.

"Wonderful will take point. The rest will be up to you. I'll still be around, but behind the scenes coordinating everything for a while."

Jazz and Dark both patted me on the back in congratulations. "You're moving up man! Congrats!"

Entice was fuming. He always had that attitude like he's supposed to have everything. He's the smartest, the strongest, the best of the group. I could tell by the way he was making fists then letting go to try to hide his anger.

"Yeah, congrats," he said through his teeth.

Maybe if Entice spent more effort being part of the team and less time sampling the product, he would have been point. He was too much of a risk, and Diamond knew it. The other guys weren't interested in leading the crew. I was thrilled to be point because that got me out of the truck and into the lead car. The lead car is more comfortable than the truck and doesn't carry product. The lead is the lookout, not the risk-taker.

"Thanks, man," I said to Diamond. "I won't let you down."

Chapter 15 - Setup

I knew Entice was pissed off. He basically quit speaking to me except when he absolutely had to. He was late to every show he didn't flat-out miss. And, he got in trouble with the law for possession.

When I heard about Entice getting arrested, I called the team for a meeting.

"I got no idea how much trouble Entice is in, but I think we shouldn't count on him for the next run," I told the crew. Diamond nodded.

"Since we are down a guy, one of you has to drive the truck," I said to Dark and Jazz. "We will just have one motorcycle backup to start this run."

Dark and Jazz decided to have a contest to see who would drive the truck. At the club that night, whoever made the least money had to drive it.

When we got to the club in Miami that night, Entire was already in the dressing room.

"Hey, man! Good to see ya! We thought you were busted," I said.

"I was. Possession. But there was only residue left in the bag, so they let me go."

"Awesome. We thought we were going to have to make the run without you."

"Nah. I'm here. Fresh and ready to go. Jail ain't nothin' for a couple days."

Dark and Jazz decided to keep the bet on and spent all night on the floor hustling. Lynette had come in that night, so I spent the evening like a boomerang trying to float and yet being drawn back into her orbit every chance I got. Money was flowing and we all made bank. We were drinking, having a good time, and making the ladies happy.

Even though it was my first night to run as point, nothing had changed except who was driving point and who was driving the truck. Everything else was business as usual, nothing to worry about. So, I didn't think about it all night.

After we shut down the club, Diamond met us in the parking lot to see us off.

"Business as usual, guys," Diamond said. "Do not drive one mile over the speed limit. Use the blinker. Don't run red lights or even yellow lights. Pay attention to the road and those around you. Keep your eyes open. Don't let each other down. You got this."

"I don't have much to say other than that," I said. "See you in Fayetteville."

I slid into the soft leather seats of my Rolls Royce and started her up. Entice was driving the truck, with Jazz and Dark following on the bikes. We headed out to I-95 for my first run as lead. I was moving up in the world.

About thirty minutes into the drive, I saw blue lights coming down the highway. I did a quick mental check. I wasn't speeding. I was wearing my seat belt. The headlights were on. The music wasn't too loud. I moved to the right to let the cop car pass by, but the blue lights followed me. Something wasn't right. I had done nothing wrong at all.

I told the other vehicle to keep moving. The last thing we wanted was for the truck to be associated with my car and get searched. Then it was over for all of us. I pulled to the shoulder, grabbed the holder from the glove box that contained my insurance, pulled my ID out of my pocket, and set both on the passenger seat. I rolled down the window and put both hands on the steering wheel so the cop could see them. Sometimes, there's just no getting around driving while Black, but you have a better chance if you seem cooperative from the start.

When the cop approached my window, he asked for my license and registration. I slowly grabbed the information I had placed on the passenger seat and handed it to the officer. He looked at my license and signaled to the other officer to come over.

"Tommy Smalls. That's the guy," he said to his partner. I checked for his name badge, but he wasn't wearing one. Shit.

"Sir, I'm going to need you to step out of the car slowly. Keep your hands where I can see them at all times, and move to the back with Officer Smith and place both hands on the trunk of the car."

I did exactly as I was told. No way Smith was his real name. He wasn't wearing a name badge either. I bet their cameras weren't on.

The first officer started searching my car. I knew that was illegal, but I didn't stop them. I didn't have anything in the car, and I didn't want to seem uncooperative. He had dug through the car for no longer than five minutes when I heard the first officer tell Officer Smith to cuff me.

I must have looked confused because Officer Smith said, "What? You think we wouldn't find it? You think you're smarter than us? You think you are badder than us?" as he cuffed me.

"I bet that's about two kilos, don't you think, Smith?"

"At least, maybe more. Jones, it's just wonderful you found it. Gotta keep these assholes off the streets."

Jones. Another fake name. I cringed at the sound of my name. Why would he say wonderful? I was just coming around to the truth that I had been set up when Jones said, "You can thank Entice for this."

Next thing I know, Jones yells," Stop! Stop!" then gives me his best right hook.

I had been set up, and I was either going to get back to my car and hope that none of this was on record yet or die on this highway. At least that punch kept Smith from getting the cuff on my other wrist. I punch Jones back and make a dash for the car door, still open thank God.

Smith yelled, "Freeze!" I didn't. I kept running for my life, and then I wasn't moving at all. Pain lashed through my body as every muscle tensed up. Tazed. I started to fall forward, but Jones, rubbing his jaw, pulled me back up and punched me again. He did have a pretty good right hook, but I barely felt it with the electricity flowing through me.

Jones pulled out his Tazer and hit me with it. Sick bastards were laughing and getting a kick out of it. I stood there staring them down for as long as I could manage. I was sweating, hot, and felt like I was going to puke. I fell to my knees. It was over. Everything was done. I was going to prison for a long, long time.

I was sucking in deep breaths of oxygen, holding myself upright as best as I could with my hand on the back of the car. All I could think about at that moment was

Lynette. At that moment, I would have given up all the money, and the cars, and the luxury just to be back in bed with her.

"What the fuck?" I heard one of the officers say. Not sure which one.

"His fucking hand is glowing!"

I was hot. Sweating. Overheating. In their confusion, they didn't even take their fingers off the triggers. They just stood there, wide-eyed, Tazing a Black man on the highway in the middle of nowhere, knowing he was set up.

I put the last bit of energy I had left into raising my head to look at my hand. Sure enough, it was glowing. The car was turning red from the heat. I wasn't doing that, was I? My hand was just inches away from the gas tank. The car started to melt. I couldn't think. Before I realized what was happening, the car blew up.

Chapter 16 – Am I Dreaming

When I started to come to, I could feel I was moving. Shit. I had no idea what in the hell had happened. I remember being Tazed. My body still hurts. It felt like I had been at the gym for three or four days straight. The rocking of the vehicle lulled me back to unconsciousness.

I'm not sure how much time had passed, but I woke again and was still confused about where I was. I couldn't move yet. Everything was stiff. I was burning up.

Burning. Somehow, I burned the car. I don't remember what the explosion sounded like, but I do remember the heat and flying through the air. Fortunately, I don't remember landing. I had been blown up.

I tried to move my feet to see if I could. I could feel and move my toes. I tried the smallest movement of my fingers. Still working. I just lay there for a minute, trying to figure out what to do.

I had been set up and blown up.

"His BP's fine. EKG looks normal. This dude is a beast to have survived that," I heard. The voice sounded muffled. My ears were ringing. *I must be in the back of an ambulance,* I thought.

I tried to remember what the back of an ambulance looked like. All I had to go off of was TV and movies. Door should be just past my feet.

"He doesn't even have any burns," I heard from my right.

"One lucky mother fucker," I heard from somewhere past my head. Probably the driver.

Everything went quiet. My instinct to run kicked back in. Without forming any real plan other than move

126

away from the voice on the right and out the door in the back, I grabbed the oxygen mask off my face, threw it to the right as I rolled off the bed to the left and down onto the floor. Then immediately rushed to the door, opened it, and jumped out.

Not the best plan I've ever come up with.

I landed on the hood of a cop car and came face to face with Officer Jones. I rolled off the hood and onto the highway. That was the worst part of this plan. My military training came in handy as I instinctually tucked and rolled to soften the blow of the fall and keep moving forward.

Nothing but trees and exits. My damaged foot hurt like a motherfucker, but I got up and ran as fast as I could toward the trees. I had to get there before the cops and EMTs figured out what was going on.

It was still pitch dark outside, so I went just a little way into the woods and climbed up a tree to use the leaves as camouflage. I was not quite within earshot to hear what was going on. The ambulance and cop car pulled off to the shoulder. It looked like one of the EMTs was checking on the cops and another was on the radio.

"No, you fucking tell Entice!" one of the officers yelled. "He is supposed to be in jail and out of the way! You fucked up our meal ticket!"

"No, you fucked this all up!"

I wasn't sure who was yelling at who, but they were pissed. Guess Entire offered them a cut to get me out of the way and then look the other way. I shimmied back down the tree and headed deeper into the woods to lay low and come up with a better plan.

Chapter 17 – Gather myself

As I lay in the grass and leaves, I knew I needed to get up and get moving, but I was still in shock.

Shock.

Through the haze of all the thoughts rushing through my brain, I remembered the electric shocks from the Tazer. I started to feel something strange happening inside my body. My muscles were starting to bulge, and my skin was glowing again. I continued to feel those shocks now. Tingles really, but the more they shocked me, the stronger they got, the stronger I got, until finally I broke free, stood up, and started running through the trees.

And then, just as suddenly as it had begun, it all stopped. The electrical shocks had caused some kind of weird reaction inside me and, when I touched the back of that car it exploded.

I had to find out what was happening to me, and I needed to do get back to Lynette.

I started walking toward the last truck stop I had passed. It was slow going because I was sore from the explosion. I had to call Lynette and tell her what had happened. I knew she would be worried about me. As I got closer to the truck stop, I could see people with cellphones. I quickly walked over and asked to call Lynette.

As we drove back to Miami, I couldn't help but think about the shots and vaccines I had been given by the military. Could those concoctions have caused something to go wrong in my body?

I wasn't sure. I hadn't heard from anyone else in my unit that strange things had happened to them, and we all got the same shots, right?

All I knew for sure was something had changed. I felt warmer and stronger than ever before. I felt the power coursing through me, and it was an exhilarating feeling.

When we got back to Lynette's place I told l her what happened, and with Lynette being a nurse I needed her help to figure out what was going on. She was more concerned about how badly I was hurt.

"I need to talk to you about something," I said. "It's kind of a long story."

"Okay, let's go inside and you can tell me all about it," she said, wrapping her arms around me.

I related the story to her from start to finish, and she listened intently.

"Do you think the Tazer could be responsible for this?" she asked when I was done.

"I don't know," I replied. "All I know is that something happened to me out there, and I need to find out what it was."

"I'll help you," she said. "We'll figure this out together."

"Baby, one thing I know for damn sure is that Entice set me up. They wanted me to get caught. But why? I don't know, and I need to find out."

"I agree, that's definitely something we need to look into," she said. "But first, let's get you cleaned up and bandaged."

I started to pull my shirt off. I was definitely sore because it hurt like hell to raise my arms over my head.

Lynette came back into the room with a clean towel and a beer.

"Oh, my God," she said as she ran to me after seeing the bruises covering my chest and arms.

"I'll be okay. I promise," I said as she handed me the beer. I took a long pull. "But first, let me take a shower."

Before I had the chance to get to the shower, she wrapped her arms around me. As we kissed, my skin started to glow again. I could feel the electricity coursing through my body, and I knew I needed to release it.

I picked her up and carried her into the bathroom, setting her down on the counter. I ripped off her clothes and started kissing my way down her body.

"Oh, Wonderful," she moaned as my mouth found her neck.

As she leaned back, she caught a glimpse of me in the mirror, glowing.

"What the hell?" she exclaimed and jumped off the counter.

I was glowing from the top of my head all the way down my spine.

It looked like my veins were filled with electricity, and it was getting brighter and brighter.

"I don't know," I said, trying to stay calm. "But whatever it is, it's happening again."

We both stood there staring at each other for a few moments, not knowing what to do.

"I need to go to Entice," I said. "I need answers."

"Okay, let's go," she said, getting dressed quickly.

"No, you need to stay here," I said. "This is something I need to do alone."

"But Wonderful, I'm worried about you," she said.

"I'll be fine. I promise," I said as I gave her a quick kiss. "If it makes you feel better, I'll stay here tonight and see if I can talk to Diamond before I go hunting for Entice."

"Okay, that sounds good," she said as she wrapped her arms around me.

I held her tight, not wanting to let go. But I knew I had to.

I wasn't sure what was going on with me, but I knew Entice had the answers to why I was targeted on the highway.

I was going to get answers, one way or another.

Chapter 18 – Warming Up

I was determined to get answers from Entice about why I was set up. I took Lynette's car, left her some money for a rental, and headed back to school. I was number one in my business class, and I was expected to give a speech at graduation.

I got back to school and tried to focus on graduation. However, it was difficult with all the thoughts running through my head. I wondered how things could have gone so wrong.

I headed over to Diamond's place and told him the entire story, leaving out the part about my glowing body causing the explosion.

"Man, that's fucked up," Diamond said. "I had no idea Entice was planning something like this. Had no idea he wasn't completely with us."

Diamond explained that Jazz and Dark had made it back with the product and reported that I had been pulled over by the cops.

"Man, I thought you had just gone to Lynette's to lay low. You didn't have anything in that car, so I didn't worry too much about you getting pulled over," Diamond said.

"Yeah, well, Entice set me up. He planted something in the car, or the cops did. I need to get to the bottom of it," I said. "I need answers."

"I hear you, man," Diamond said. "But be careful. Entice is a dangerous dude. I'll reach out to some of my contacts and see if I can find out what the hell is going on."

"Thanks, man," I said as I headed out the door. "I gotta be here this week, but I'm heading to Miami right after graduation. I'll meet you there late Saturday night.

I'm taking this to the limit."

"You do what you gotta do, man, and I'll do what I've gotta do," Diamond said. He was on the phone before I was out the door.

Chapter 19 – The Report

While speaking with a reliable source from Miami police, I learned that Sunday morning, the two police officers and the ambulance crew were called into the police headquarters to give their account of what happened on the highway with the explosion.

The room was silent as they waited for someone to say something. Finally, the chief spoke up. "criminal got away?" he asked incredulously. "How did that happen?"

The officers and ambulance crew looked at each other, unsure of who should speak first. Finally, one of the officers spoke up. "I'm sorry, sir. We will find him," he said shamefully.

"Yes, you will," the chief said. "But first, I want an explanation as to why I have to buy a new police car and fix a ambulance after a traffic stop."

The officer took a deep breath and began to explain what happened. "We pulled him over after we got a tip he was running drugs. Sure enough, he was carrying. He tried to take off, so we deployed the Taser in order to arrest him."

The room went silent again.

The chief was trying to process what he had just been told. "So, let me get this straight. You Tased him and he blew up my police car?"

"I'm sorry, sir," the officer said sheepishly.

"Try again," the chief said.

One of the EMTs mumbled under his breath, "He was glowing."

"What was that?" the chief asked.

"He was glowing," the EMT said a little louder. "When he was in the back of the ambulance, he was unconscious, and then he just started to, I don't know, glow."

"Did you say he was glowing?" the chief asked incredulously.

"Yes, sir," the EMT said. "It was like he had a light inside of him."

"What did you do?" the chief asked.

"We, um, we covered him up with a blanket and then he just exploded," the officer said.

"He just exploded?" the chief asked.

"Yes, sir," the officer said. "The ambulance, everything just blew up."

"So, he's some kind of superhuman then?" the chief asked. "I find that hard to believe."

"I don't know, sir," the officer said. "But whatever he is, we need to find him."

"Why don't we try this one more time," this chief said. "This time, let's try the truth."

No one spoke. They all just stared at the table.

The chief slammed his fist on the table. "Find him!" he yelled. "Find him now! And bring in this genius with the tip."

Chapter 20 – Need Answers

Sometimes it's hard for people to enjoy their life, worrying about what others have. I guess things would have been so much easier if I'd been arrested like he wanted me to. Fortunately, corrupt cops are usually stupid cops.

When Entice had called the officers Sunday morning and found out that I wasn't in jail, he was livid.

"What the hell do you mean he got away?" he yelled.

"He blew up our car. And the ambulance," one of the officers said.

"I handed him to you in gold handcuffs," Entice said. "All you had to do was put him in the back of the car, drive him to the station, and lock him up. How difficult is that?"

"He's a criminal mastermind," the officer said, debating telling Entice about the glow. "We're not used to dealing with someone like him."

"You're goddamn right you're not used to dealing with someone like him," Entice said. "Because if you were, he would be in jail right now."

Entice slammed the phone down, then picked it up and called the officer back.

"How do you plan on finding him?" Entice asked before the officer said a word.

"Until he comes back to Miami, there isn't anything we can do. We don't have jurisdiction," the officer said.

"Lynette," Entice thought out loud. "I'm sure he will head straight for Lynette's. Find her, you find him."

When Lynette returned to Miami on Friday, the officers were there to greet her at the airport.

"Ma'am, you need to come with us. There has been an incident with Wonderful."

"What incident?" Lynette asked.

"We tried to arrest him last weekend. He escaped from our custody, and we believe he might be headed to your house."

"Why would he come to my house?" Lynette asked, trying to keep calm.

"You are his girlfriend, right? Wonderful is armed and very dangerous. We need to take you to a safe location to ensure your safety."

Lynette started to protest that she was safe, but the officers each grabbed one of her arms and hauled her out of the airport and into their police car.

Now, Lynette was tied up and blindfolded at Entice's cousin's house.

Lynette's phone buzzed, and one of the officers picked it up checking her text message.

"Hey babe. Don't forget graduation tomorrow. Sorry work kept you from making it. See you Monday morning. Love you."

Chapter 21 – Plan B

I was nervous. It was the night before my last set of exams, and I had a lot to do. But there was something else on my mind that was distracting me from my work.

I had been trying to find Entice all week, but I just couldn't track him down.

I finally finished up my work and headed out for a drive in the hopes of finding Entice. As I drove, I felt angrier and angrier. I wanted answers, and I was going to get them.

Finally, graduation day arrived. I walked across the stage and accepted my diploma with pride. As I looked out into the audience, I saw Entice standing in the back of the convention center. Keeping a cool head, I hurried down the stairs, heading toward Entice.

"You set me up!" I murmured as I grabbed Entice by the collar.

"I don't know what you're talking about," Entice said calmly.

"You were the one who told those cops to stop on the highway! Why?" I demanded.

"You haven't figured that out yet?" Entice asked. "How is a college boy so stupid?"

"What are you talking about?"

"You have something I want," Entice said. "And I will stop at nothing to get it."

"What do you want?"

"Your power," Entice said. "I want your power."

I stopped dead in my tracks. Did Entice know about the glow? "Power? What power?"

"I should have been lead. Not you," Entice said. "I've been doing all the grunt work for years. I should be the one taking over for Diamond. I've earned it."

I sighed with relief. Entice was just acting like any other fool who just wants to be on top.

"Diamond chose me because you are an unpredictable hothead," I said. "But trust me, not only are you never going to be lead, you are out, and I'm going to make sure that you pay for what you did to me."

I looked down and noticed my hands were starting to glow again. I quickly shoved them in my pockets.

"We'll see about that," Entice said. "I'm going to enjoy watching you suffer."

Entice turned and walked away as I stood there, shocked. I had no idea what I was up against, but I was going to find out. And I was going to make Entice pay.

"The next time I see you will be the last time I see you," I said, so calmly I scared myself.

Entice stopped and turned around, "By the way, we got your girl."

Chapter 22 - Hotter

I went straight from graduation to my car and headed for the airport. I hated flying, but I needed to get to Miami quickly. I called my mother on the way to the airport and apologized for missing out on the rest of the celebration. I tried to call Lynette over and over, but she didn't pick up the phone.

My anger was starting to bubble over, and my hands started glowing again.

Calm down, Wonderful, I told myself. *Save it for Entice.*

I headed straight for the police station when I arrived in Miami and demanded to talk to the chief.

When I didn't get anywhere, I told the officer at the desk who I was and assured him the chief would want to speak to me. I found myself in handcuffs in an interview room still waiting to speak to someone two hours later.

When officers did come in, it was Dumb and Dumber who had pulled me over. Before they could start the bad-cop, bad-cop routine, I said, "I'll tell you everything, but I will only talk to the chief."

"Nah, we'll just take you back to a cell," the first officer, the one that called himself Smith, said.

"I'll take it from here. Donovan, Juarez, out. Grab us some coffee please," the chief said as he walked in the door.

After the officers left, Chief Martinez sat down at the table.

"So, you are the guy who blew up my vehicles. Care to explain?"

I took a deep breath. "First off, I didn't do that. I have no real explanation for that. Maybe your officers did it to cover their tracks. I was set up."

The chief interrupted. "Oh! I didn't realize you were set up. That changes everything. Let me get you out of those cuffs and on your way!" He stood up, pounded the table and yelled, "You are a drug runner who blew up a police car and an ambulance. You are looking at a very long time behind bars. You better start telling the truth."

"Check my phone. Look for a text message from Diamond right at the top," I said.

The chief pulled my phone out of the manila envelope on the table and opened up the messages.

"Spoke with an officer at Miami PD. Said she had heard of the arrest. Cops are Juarez and Donavan. Overheard Juarez on the phone while someone was yelling at him about how they screwed up a drug plant."

"You have my attention," the chief said.

I explained that the man on the other end of the line was Entice. We were part of a dance group that traveled between North Carolina and Miami doing shows, but Entice was jealous because Diamond was giving me the best stage times. The truth wasn't going to help him in any way.

"I was headed back to North Carolina to attend my graduation. I was top of my class. Check my photos," I told the chief.

The chief switched over to the photos on my phone. The last few were of me holding my award, wearing my cap and gown, hugging my mother and posing with family before the graduation ceremony.

"Did you have drugs in the car?" the chief asked.

"No, sir. I left for North Carolina right after our show in Miami last weekend to get back in time for finals and graduation. I don't do drugs."

Chief called on his radio and asked records to bring him anything they had on Entice.

"Entice set me up," I continued. "Those cops were in on it, and now they have my girl. Entice showed up at my graduation ceremony. I almost lost it when I confronted him, and he said he had my girl."

"You watch too much *CSI: Miami*," the chief said.

There was a knock on the door, and an officer handed the chief a file folder. He looked through a few things and asked me to hang tight before walking out the door.

The chief walked into the screening room where Donavan and Juarez had been watching the interview. They both looked worried.

"So, you guys arrested this guy Entice a few weeks ago, but he was let out based on, according to your report, providing valuable information leading to a drug bust."

"Yes, sir. He tipped us off about him running drugs," Donavan said as he pointed to me in the room.

"Thing is, this report is dated two weeks before the stop. How did you know it would lead to a drug bust two weeks later?" the chief asked.

"Must have been a typo," Juarez said.

"I'm not so sure," the chief said as he looked at me

and then back to the officers. "He looks calm and confident while you two are sweating bullets. I think it's time you start telling the truth."

The chief called back to records and asked for the radio calls from the two officers from the day of my arrest through that day.

Knowing they were caught, Juarez said, "We didn't plant anything."

"Shut up," Donavan whispered.

"Entice told us this guy was the head of their group and that he was just a lackey loading stuff into trucks and unloading it. So, we followed the tip. He was right. We found drugs."

"What did you find?" the chief asked.

"It looked like a gram, maybe," Juarez said. "Cocaine."

"That's a class-three felony, but only five years. Even taking on destruction of public property won't add much. If you really think this guy is a kingpin, we need more to put him away."

"Sir," the chief's radio chirped. "There are no dash cam videos or personal camera videos from the arrest. The radio has the call-in, but then it goes to static. I'm pulling the rest of the records now. It will take me about an hour."

"So, no evidence either. I'm going to cut him loose. You two keep an eye on him and see if he leads you anywhere. I'm putting an undercover unit on him, too. Get some evidence!"

Chapter 23 – Game Face

I left the police station, rubbing my wrists from the cuffs. I jumped into my rental car and headed for Lynette's house.

When I got there, I let myself in and looked around. She wasn't there. Her purse wasn't there. I checked the closet, and her suitcase wasn't there. Lynette always unpacked and put her suitcase back in the hall closet when she got home.

She hadn't even made it home. I tried calling her again, and this time it went straight to voicemail.

I called Diamond. "Entice has Lynette. Any idea where he may have taken her?"

"You can try his aunt's, his sister's, and his cousin's places. But man, he'd be stupid to take her to family. They are the only ones I know of that still live in Miami, but I don't have addresses."

"Thanks, Diamond," I said, then hung up the phone and grab my gun.

As I left Lynette's, I noticed a police car parked down the street. A tail.

Instead of trying to find Lynette, I came up with a plan. I stopped at a local Mexican restaurant and was shown to a table. Sure enough, while I was waiting for the waitress, the cop car drove through the lot.

"We need to go check on the girl. He's gonna be here at least thirty minutes or so," Donavan said.

"Let's split up. I'll take you back to the station to get your car. It's just a couple of miles away. You go check on the girl, and I'll come back and keep an eye on him, let you know when he leaves," Juarez said.

"Sounds like a plan."

As soon as I saw the cop car pull out of the lot and

leave, I dropped a $50 bill on the table and left without ordering. Now, I was following them.

The officers split up at the station, and one of them got in a regular car. I couldn't follow both. I watched as both cars pulled out of the lot. The cop car headed back in the direction of the restaurant while the other one headed in the opposite direction. I made a split-second decision and decided to follow the regular car.

About twenty minutes later, the car pulled up in front of a house and the officer went in. I parked a couple of houses down and waited.

I grabbed my gun from the glove box and started making my way slowly and quietly to the house across the street. Standing in the side yard, I could see the officer at the back door talking to a woman. In the background, I thought I saw Lynette.

I walked around to the front door and knocked. Nobody answered, but I could hear voices inside. I tried the knob, and it was unlocked. I slowly opened the door and peeked in.

There, in the living room, Lynette was tied to a chair with duct tape over her mouth. Officer Donavan was standing next to her with a cup of coffee in his hand.

"I'm glad you're here," the officer said. "This girl has been giving me a hard time."

"Let her go," I said as I stepped into the room and aimed my gun at the officer.

"Now why would I do that?" the officer asked. "She's worth a lot of money to the right person. You."

"I don't care how much money she is worth. Let her go now."

""No can do," the officer said as he reached for his gun.

I shot him before he could get it out of the holster. The officer fell to the ground, dead. I rushed to Lynette and started untying her.

"Are you okay?" I asked as I pulled the duct tape off her mouth.

"I am now," she said as she threw her arms around my neck and kissed me. "Thank you."

I untied Lynette from the chair and helped her to her feet.

"Let's get out of here," she said.

"Not just yet," I said, and looked at the woman standing in her living room, staring at the man bleeding out on the floor. She started screaming.

I tossed Lynette the rope and gag that they'd used on her. "Care to return the favor?" he asked her.

Lynette laughed. "Oh yes, I would."

While Lynette tied up the woman, who had starting yelling that the police would make us pay for this, no trial, no jury, we would just disappear, I tried to figure out what to do next.

"Baby, we just need to go," Lynette said. "We have

to go now before more cops show up."

"I know. But Entice is still out there. I still want answers."

I pulled the gag from the woman's mouth.

"Who are you?" I asked her.

"Screw you," she said and tried to spit at him. "You just killed my husband."

Lynette stepped forward and slapped the shit out of the woman.

"He was going to kill us both," Lynette said.

The woman just glared at her.

"Where is Entice?" I asked.

"I don't know what you're talking about," she said and turned her head away from him.

I sighed and put the gag back in her mouth. I looked at Lynette. "We need to go."

"I know," she said as she took my hand. "Wait. Cop car is pulling up out front."

"Crap. Go back in one of the bedrooms," Wonderful said. "I'll handle this."

I stood just to the side of the door and waited for Officer Juarez to walk in.

"What the hell, man? I've been trying to call you for twenty," Juarez stopped and stared at his partner, lying dead on the floor.

I stepped from behind the door and put my gun to Juarez's head.

"You're next, man, if you don't start talking."

"What the hell happened here?" Juarez asked.

"I asked you a question first," I said. "Where is Entice?"

"I don't know what you're talking about," Juarez said.

I cocked my gun. "Try again."

"He's on his way back from North Carolina. Should be arriving at the airport any minute."

"You're sure he's on his way back here?"

"Yes. His flight is due in at 4:30."

I looked at my watch. It was 4:40.

"Call him. Tell him I came looking for Lynette and now you have me, too."

"But," Juarez started to protest.

"Do you really want to end up like your partner over there?"

"Okay, okay. I'm going to reach for my phone."

"Wait up a sec," I said, and reached over and unclipped the officer's service weapon and putting it in the back of his jeans.

"Okay, get your phone."

I listened as Juarez called Entice and told him that he was at Donovan's house with the girl and Wonderful.

"He's on his way," Juarez said eventually, hanging up his phone.

"I don't really need you anymore, but I might let

163

you live," I said. "If you can make this all go away. I know you cops can do that."

Juarez looked at his partner on the floor. "Man, I got kids and a wife."

"Just make it go away, and I'll let you live," I offered.

"Yeah. I'll make it go away," Juarez sighed.

"Perfect. Now, we wait."

Chapter 24 – The Beginning

I went back over to the tied-up woman and removed her gag.

"What's your name?"

"Screw you."

"What's your name?" I asked again, calmly.

"Rebecca," she said.

"Look, Rebecca, I'm going to untie you here in just a bit. When Entice gets here, I want you to let him in."

Tears started flowing down her face. "I don't want to help you."

"I'm really sorry you got mixed up in all of this. But your husband was a crooked cop. He had me arrested because he's greedy and wanted money."

"I know," she said. "I know he is—was—a bad cop. But I still loved him. Well, I thought I did, anyway, until he showed up with that girl and told me to keep her tied up and keep an eye on her. I don't want to be involved in any of this."

"Look, you let Entice in, and that's all you need to do. Juarez over here promised to make all this go away. You can start over. Find someone better."

Rebecca looked again at her husband.

"Look at her arms, Wonderful," Lynette said.

I pushed up her sleeves. Her arms were black and blue. "He was kind of a jerk," Rebecca said. "I'll let him in, but that's it. Nothing else."

"Nothing else," I said as I untied her.

About thirty minutes later, Entice pulled into the driveway. I nodded at Rebecca, who went to open the door. She let Entice in and then ran out the door and down the street.

The first thing Entice saw when he entered the house was Juarez, tied up. Then, he noticed Donavan dead on the floor.

"What the hell happened?" Entice started.

"I know you set me up," I said with my gun pointed at Entice as I walked out of the back bedroom.

"Yeah, well," Entice started to say as he reached for his gun. I didn't wait. I shot at Entice, hitting him in the shoulder.

Entice looked at Juarez. "This is your fault, man. If you weren't such a fucking idiot. You better fix this. I will hunt you down and kill you if you don't."

Entice tried to lift his gun up to shoot me, but the shot went wild because he couldn't move his arm.

Juarez finally managed to get the ropes loose on his arms, tipped the chair over, grabbed Entice's gun, and shot at me, hitting me three times in the chest.

As I fell to my knees, looking at the officer in disbelief, I felt myself start to glow.

"Oh shit, not again," Juarez said.

"What the … ," Entice started.

"Get me out of here," Juarez screamed at Entice.

As the glow spread throughout my body, I was lifted off the ground as the bullets were pushed from my body and the wounds sealed up.

I looked at Lynette, who had run in from the back room when she heard the shots. As soon as my hand touched the floor, flames like solar flares shot out and spread across the floor, igniting everything in their path.

"Come on, baby, let's get out of here."

"You got it," Lynette said as she grabbed my hand and headed for the car.

As we drove off, we heard sirens in the distance and saw Rebecca staring in horror from across the street as the house burned to the ground.

Made in the USA
Columbia, SC
05 April 2024